WAIT!

DON'T CLOSE THE BOOK!

THERE'S MORE!

FIND MORE:

Games & Puzzles
Heroes & Villains
Authors & Illustrators

D0009195

www.CAPSTONEKIDS.com

More Tales to Treasure

Open a Storybook Classic and experience the world of traditional fairy tales told through simple prose and splendid artwork. These safe and inventive picture books feature beautiful and whimsical illustrations that will charm young and old alike.

STORYBOOK Classics

THE 3 LITTLE PIGS

Snow White

Hansel and Gretel

Cinderella

Puss in Boots

little Red Riding Hood

GOLDILOCKS and the Three Bears

Picture Window Books
Minneapolis, Minnesota

First published in the United States in 2010
by Picture Window Books
A Capstone Imprint
151 Good Counsel Drive
P.O. Box 669
Mankato, Minnesota 56002
www.capstonepub.com

©2008, Edizioni El S.r.l., Treiste Italy in RICCIOLI D'ORO E I TRE ORSI

Printed in the United States of America in North Mankato, Minnesota.
032010 005718R

All books published by Picture Window Books
are manufactured with paper containing
at least 10 percent post-consumer waste.

Library of Congress Cataloging-in-Publication Data
Piumini, Roberto.
[Riccioli d'Oro e i tre orsi. English]
Goldilocks and the three bears / by Roberto Piumini; illustrated by Valentina Salmaso.
p. cm. — (Storybook classics)
ISBN 978-1-4048-5499-4 (library binding)
[1. Folklore. 2. Bears—Folklore.] I. Salmaso, Valentina, ill. II. Goldilocks
and the three bears. English. III. Title.
PZ8.1.P688Go 2010
398.22—dc22
[E]   2009010421

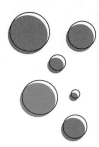

GOLDILOCKS
and the
Three Bears

Retold by Roberto Piumini

Illustrated by Valentina Salmaso

Once upon a time, three bears lived in a house in the forest. There was a little bear, a medium-sized bear, and a great big bear.

Everything in their house had three sizes. The little bear ate from a little bowl, the medium-sized bear ate from a medium-sized bowl, and the great big bear ate from a great big bowl.

One day, the three bears cooked a steaming pot of porridge. After letting it simmer for a while, they poured it into their bowls.

"It's still too hot to eat," said the great big bear.

"If we taste it now, we will burn our tongues!" said the little bear.

"Let's go for a walk under the trees while it cools," said the medium-sized bear.

So they went outside to go for a walk in the forest.

While the three bears were gone, a little girl named Goldilocks came upon their house. First, she looked through the window. Then she peeped through the keyhole. When she saw that nobody was home, she turned the doorknob and slowly opened the door. As she stepped inside, she saw the three bowls of porridge sitting on the table.

Goldilocks was very hungry. Without stopping to think, she tasted the porridge in the great big bowl.

"This porridge is too hot to eat," she said.

Then she tasted the porridge in the medium-sized bowl. "And this porridge is too cold," she said.

Finally, she tried the porridge in the littlest bowl. "This porridge is just right!" she said, and she quickly ate it all up.

After Goldilocks had eaten, she decided to sit down for a while. She climbed onto the great big chair. "Oh! This chair is too hard," she said.

Then she tried sitting on the medium-sized chair. "Oh! This chair is too soft," she grumbled.

Finally she sat on the little chair, and it was just right! But Goldilocks was too big for it, and the chair broke into little pieces.

Goldilocks decided it was time for a nap. She brushed herself off and went upstairs to the bedroom, where she found three beds.

Goldilocks tried to pull herself up to the great big bed. "This bed is too tall for me to climb!" she said.

Then she laid down on the medium-sized bed. "And this bed is too fluffy," she said.

Finally, she climbed onto the littlest bed. "This bed is just right!" she said, and she fell right to sleep.

A short while later, the three bears decided to return home to eat their porridge. Once inside, they noticed that someone else had been there.

"Who tasted my porridge?" the great big bear said, when he saw the spoon in his bowl.

The medium-sized bear saw that his spoon was in his porridge too.

"And who has tasted my porridge?" he said.

Then the little bear saw his bowl was empty.

"Someone has tasted my porridge too!" he cried. "And they ate it all up!"

The great big bear turned to the other bears. "Let's look for our uninvited visitor," he said.

Soon the great big bear saw that the cushion on his chair had been moved.

"Who has been sitting in my chair?" he asked.

The medium-sized bear saw that his cushion was wrinkled.

"Who has been sitting in my chair?" he wondered.

Then the little bear saw what had happened to his chair.

"Someone sat in my chair too!" cried the little bear. "And they broke it into tiny little pieces!"

Even more concerned now, the great big bear said, "Let's look upstairs."

One by one, ever so slowly, the three bears climbed up the stairs into their bedroom.

On the big tall bed, the sheets were pulled to one side. "Someone tried to climb onto my bed!" cried the great big bear.

On the medium-sized bed, the blanket was wrinkled. "Someone has been in my bed!" cried the medium-sized bear.

Then the little bear saw a little girl sleeping in his little bed.

"Someone has been in my bed too!" cried the little bear. "And she's sleeping right there!"

All three bears roared, "Who is this little girl who's sleeping in our house?"

One voice alone would have been enough to wake up Goldilocks. Three voices together, of course, scared her and startled her from her nap.

When Goldilocks saw the three bears looking at her, her eyes and her mouth opened wide. Instead of crying out, she quickly jumped off the bed, leaped out the window, and fell into a big soft bush. Then, without stopping for even a second, she ran away as fast as she could.

The medium-sized bear let out a sigh. "We will have to fix little bear's chair," he said.

"And we will have to lock the door when we go outside from now on," added the great big bear.

"I'm so hungry," said the little bear. "Can I have some of your porridge, please?" he pleaded.

With a great big sigh, the three bears went back downstairs.

And Goldilocks? She just kept running.

FAIRY TALE
Follow-Up

1. Why did Goldilocks decide to go into the three bears' house? Would you go into someone's house uninvited?

2. Do you think Goldilocks is a good girl? Do you think she is naughty? Explain your answer.

3. How do you think the three bears felt when they realized someone had been in their home while they were out?

4. What lesson did the bears learn?

5. What lesson did Goldilocks learn?

Glossary

cushion (KUSH-uhn)—a type of pillow used to make a chair more comfortable

grumbled (GRUHM-buhld)—complained in a grouchy way

porridge (POR-ij)—a breakfast food made by boiling oats in milk or water until it is thick

simmer (SIM-ur)—to boil very gently

uninvited (uhn-in-VIE-tid)—not asked to come in or go someplace

wrinkled (RING-kuhld)—messed up, so there are lines in a piece of fabric

Fairy tales have been told for hundreds of years. Most fairy tales share certain elements, or pieces. Once you learn about these elements, you can try writing your own fairy tales.

Element 1: The Characters

Characters are the people, animals, or other creatures in the story. They can be good or evil, silly or serious. Can you name the characters in *Goldilocks and the Three Bears*? Here's a hint — they are all listed in the title. Goldilocks, the great big bear, the middle-sized bear, and the little bear.

Element 2: The Setting

The setting tells us *when* and *where* a story takes place. The *when* of the story could be a hundred years ago or a hundred years in the future. There may be more than one *where* in a story. You could go from a house to a school to a park. In *Goldilocks and the Three Bears*, the story says it happened "once upon a time." Usually this means that it takes place many years ago. And *where* does it take place? At the bears' home in the forest.

Element 3: The Plot

Think about what happens in the story. You are thinking about the plot, or the action of the story. In fairy tales, the action begins nearly right away. In *Goldilocks and the Three Bears*, the plot begins when the three bears cook their porridge and discover it is too hot to eat. The middle-sized bear says, "Let's go for a walk under the trees while it cools." And the story takes off from there!

Element 4: Magic

Did you know that all fairy tales have an element of magic? The magic is what makes a fairy tale different from other stories. Often, the magic comes in the form of a character that doesn't exist in real life, such as a giant, a witch, or in the case of *Goldilocks and the Three Bears*, talking animals.

Element 5: A Happy Ending

Years ago, fairy tales ended on a sad note, but today, most fairy tales have a happy ending. Did *Goldilocks and the Three Bears* have a happy ending? Sure! Even though they needed to fix little bear's chair, the three bears were once again happy and comfortable in their own home, ready to eat their bowls of porridge.

Now that you know the basic elements of a fairy tale, try writing your own! Create characters, both good and bad. Decide when and where their story will take place to give them a setting. Now put them into action during the plot of the story. Don't forget that you need some magic! And finally, give the hero of your story a happy ending.

ABOUT THE Author

Roberto Piumini lives and works in Italy. He has worked with children as both a teacher and a theater actor/entertainer. He credits these experiences for inspiring the youthful language of his many books. With his crisp and imaginative way of dealing with every kind of subject, he keeps charming his young readers. His award-winning books, for both children and adults, have been translated into many languages.

ABOUT THE Illustrator

As a small child, Valentina Salmaso enjoyed making art, especially in the kitchen. Today, she loves to draw and illustrate for children. Her work has been published internationally. Valentina remains a little girl in her heart. She loves to travel, and when she illustrates, she lets her imagination take her places she can only dream of.